DO ZEBRAS BLOOM
IN THE SPRING?

Library of Congress Cataloging-in-Publication Data

Woodworth, Viki.
Does a zebra bloom in spring? / Viki Woodworth.
p. cm
Summary: Simple, humorous rhymes ask a series of questions
about things that appear in the spring.
ISBN 1-56766-220-X (hard cover : lib. bd.)
[1. Summer—Fiction. 2. Stories in rhyme.]
1. Title.
PZ8.3.W893Doz 1996   95-44679
[E]—dc20   CIP / AC

DO ZEBRAS BLOOM IN THE SPRING?

by Viki Woodworth

Viki Woodworth and family.

A violin?
A crown?
A plant
or a trout?

(A plant)

What buds and blooms
in the warm spring air?

A zebra?
A tree?

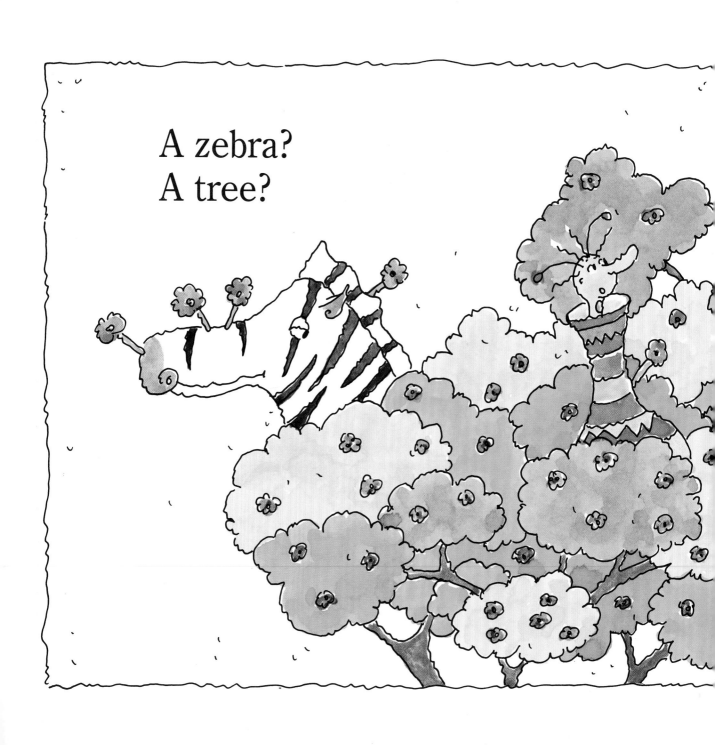

A vase
or a bear?

(A tree)

An umbrella?
A pot?
A frog
or a jeep?

(A frog)

Who hatches from an egg
in the early spring?

A chair?
An artist?

A bird
or a king?

(A bird)

The sunshine and rain,
which we all know,

make spring
the season

when new
things grow.